This Gentle Land

This Gentle Land

Growing up in the 1930's and 40's

Ruth Stewart

iUniverse, Inc.
New York Lincoln Shanghai

This Gentle Land
Growing up in the 1930's and 40's

Copyright © 2007 by Ruth Stewart

iUniverse books may be ordered through booksellers or by contacting:

iUniverse
2021 Pine Lake Road, Suite 100
Lincoln, NE 68512
www.iuniverse.com
1-800-Authors (1-800-288-4677)

ISBN: 978-0-595-47263-5 (pbk)
ISBN: 978-0-595-91538-5 (ebk)

Printed in the United States of America

Dedicated to my mother, Alma Creech Lassiter; and in memory of my father, Blake Lassiter.

Also dedicated to my sisters, Shirley Huffman, Sylvia Woody, Sue Wood, Linda Waddell, and brother Max Lassiter; to my husband, Don Stewart, and to my dear friend Mary Alice Wightman. They all encouraged me throughout the writing of this book.

Contents

ACKNOWLEDGMENT

I gratfully acknowledge the help of Lewis Mullen, photographer of the cover picture and the landscape pictures of the farm.

INTRODUCTION

Two mules slowly pull a plow
down a furrow curving through a disked field.
The man walking behind the plow focuses
on the plowshare as it folds the land back
on itself to prepare the soil for planting.
For thousands of years man has labored
by hand in the soil to produce
food for his family.
This man, however stands on the cusp
of change. Soon machines will do what a thousand
laborers did. The Industrial Revolution
will lure young people away from small family
farms to cities and towns where there is
more lucrative work. These farms will become an
integral part of large agribusinesses. Other farms
will grow houses instead of crops.
This is the story of one farm and its resident
family, who laughed and loved and hurt
through floods and droughts, heat and cold
to sustain a living in the good earth.
Its story is legion; just like thousands
of other farm families throughout America.

This story is only unique because it is the story
of my parents, my siblings; because it is my story.

Blake and Alma Lassiter, the early years.

THE INHERITANCE

The year was 1930.
The day was October 20, crisp, cool and sun drenched.
The lane sloping gently up to the eastern North Carolina
farm was flanked
by trees in brilliant
colors of fall.
It had been a lovely simple wedding,
and now Blake and Alma Creech Lassiter were coming home.
The 125-acre farm of gently rolling
hills of sandy loam
was a gift from Blake's father,
James Lassiter, who
collected farms like other farmers collected
machinery. He bought them
to give to each of his five children
when they got ready to "get out on their own."
Blake had been tending this land
for several years
while still living with his parents.
The clapboard farmhouse on the property contained six
rooms, with a front porch running the
width of the house.
Iva, Blake's younger sister had come
earlier and "spruced up" the house for the newlyweds.
At this time the country was in the throes

of the Great Depression.
Times would be tough; but on this
delightful day
Alma and Blake were confident
they could make it.

THE FIRST SIX YEARS 1930–1936

Somehow Alma and Blake
made it through the worst
of the Great Depression.
They were grateful to be living
on a farm where they could grow most of the food
they needed.
After they were married awhile,
Max was born.
He had a head full of black
hair
and an incurable
curiosity.
Max loved exploring his world.
He was a world class crawler.
One day he was crawling under the house,
and a nail protruding
from the floorboards
drew a torrent
of blood
from his scalp.
Mama was sure
she had lost her firstborn.
He survived however, to
adventure again.
The southern-fried drumstick was
Max's all-time favorite
food. When
Max saw a hen one day
in the chicken yard, he chased her

crying, "Hen hen, I want bone."
When Max was one
Shirley
was born.
When Shirley was two
I was born.
The year was 1934.
While Mama kept an eye
on ever-curious
Max,
Shirley and I enjoyed
digging in drawers and closets,
pulling out treasures,
cutting each other's hair,
playing dress-up
with dolls,
and anything else that made a big mess.
"I can't have a thing,"
Mama said in desperation. But
she never seemed real desperate,
Because
she kept letting us
pull apart the house;
and she kept putting it
back
together again.

SYLVIA, SUE AND LINDA ARRIVE

When I was three
Sylvia was born.
When Sylvia was two
Sue was born.
When Sue was one
Linda was born, and I was six.
Linda's birth is the first one
I remember.
On that hot August day all five
of us were taken
to visit Aunt Iva
and Uncle Grover who lived up another
hill from us.
Aunt Iva fixed us some ice-cold lemonade.
After awhile
Daddy came and got us.
I jumped up on the
running board of the car
to hear the promised "surprise."
We all gathered around Daddy
and heard that a brand new baby
named Linda Creech had arrived.
She was so sweet and pretty and chubby
that Max called her
a little angel!

Max as a baby.

Shirley and Ruth.

Sylvia and Linda.

Sue and Linda.

FULL HOUSE

Well now the house
was full. With six children there was
plenty of work to be done.
While Daddy tended the farm,
Mama was busy cooking, cleaning, ironing, gardening,
washing clothes, preparing bottles, potty
training, sewing, sorting, and mending.
She was happy doing it all;
But a little help was
growing along.
As he got old enough, Max began
to help Daddy with such outside chores
as giving the mules grain and hay,
and feeding the hogs. He even learned
to milk the cow.
Shirley helped Mama with her many chores
in the house,
while I began to help Daddy by
feeding the chickens.
Later Sylvia joined Daddy and me.
I guess Sue and Linda
filled in wherever they
were needed.

A ROAD RUNS THROUGH IT

Our farm was cut in half
by a one lane dirt
road that ran in front of our house.
It ended at a pond on
one end, and the road to Four Oaks
at the other end
near a creek called Sassarizer.
It didn't much matter
that the road was narrow,
because not too many cars
met on that stretch of packed dirt.
Our house, painted white, was
dwarfed by a grove of huge
oak trees. I guess those oak trees
were here when the Mayflower docked.
And that in itself
bequeathed to us
a sense of history, giving
this piece of land
a special importance.
On the pond end, a rattley, plank bridge
stretched across our road.
From our house we could hear
a car rumbling across the bridge.
We would run to the front yard
to see who was passing!

THE WELL

Out under the oak trees
near the road,
was an old well.
Above the well-hole dangled
a rope which held a bucket.
I liked to stand on tiptoes
and peek over the well enclosure
to look into that deep, mysterious hole
with water shining like a big silver dollar.
If Mama was around she'd
always say,
"Be careful, Ruth. Don't fall in."
Why, I don't know.
There was no way I could
climb that well enclosure,
which was as high as my head!
The thing which made that well even more
mysterious was Max's claim
(He vowed it was true) that if
you held a mirror above the well, you could see
the person you would marry. I fell for
that one.
I sneaked a mirror from Mama's
dresser, and tilted it just right
to reflect the water below.
When I peeked at
the mirror to see who I would marry,

I saw a face,
and it was mine!

THE BARN

Across the road
from the well
and house
sat a big, rambling, unpainted barn with
a mule lot connected.
Pieces of plows, droppings of hay,
and plowshares Daddy
planned to use someday, were scattered around.
There were also buckets,
mule harnesses, and other items
too numerous to mention, lying on the ground
in front of the barn.
Piles of soft, prickly hay
filled the top floor of the barn.
We begged to play there,
But Mama wouldn't let us.
I guess she
was afraid we'd fall
through the opening in the floor
which Daddy used to poke
forkfulls of hay down to the mules.
In fact, Mama never liked
that barn
right in front of the
house.
She'd say,"Blake,
why don't you tear down that ugly thing,
and build another one somewhere else?"

And he'd say, "I plan to, Alma."
And one day he did.

WHERE THE POKEBERRIES GREW

Behind the old barn
in an overgrown wild place
the pokeberries grew in abundance.
It was a special place
to play at certain times of the year,
when clusters of deep purple berries
hung in lusious burgundy temptation.
Now we had been sufficiently warned
not to eat those berries.
Mama told us horror stories about
children dying with
stomachaches
or paralysis so bad
their eyes "froze" open.
However, there were plenty of
other things
to do with the juice
of those pokeberries.
We painted our fingernails
and our toenails,
and the fingernails and toenails
of our dolls.
We made concoctions
the color of wine
and fed it to our "di dee dolls."
The dolls especially liked
the pokeberry pies!

THE PATH

Beside the barn
a path
split the fields in two.
If you followed the path
all the way
through the fields,
then along the margin of the woods,
you would come to
a little unpainted,
rough-sided
house.
It sat in a copse of tall pines
that seemed to sing
when the wind stirred them.
Mr. and Mrs. Stanley lived there.
Mr. Stanley made a living caning chair seats.
I sometimes visited them.
They were very nice.
I suppose Daddy gave them this place to live
because they were old.
They gave me sassafras tea
to drink.
It tasted awful.
They had a tremendously high feather bed;
and they let Shirley and me spend
the night sleeping on it.
It was quite an experience!
When Shirley and I sank

down into the feather mattress,
it almost enveloped us.

EXPANDING

While all of us children
were growing,
Daddy was busy building extra room
for everyone.
He closed in the side porch
for a sitting room.
He somehow found a place
for another bedroom, adding and dividing
with the help of a carpenter
named Mr. Barnes.
Mr. Barnes was a big tease;
and we hung around them while they
were working
just to hear him "carry on."
He also helped Daddy
build a washhouse, so Mama would
have a place for a washing machine
and three tubs to rinse
the clothes.
They built another room onto
the washhouse. We called that room
the "kettle room."
In the kettle room Daddy and Mr. Barnes enclosed
a huge black iron pot in brick,
leaving a space underneath for a fire
to heat the water.
Mama used this pot to boil the white clothes
on wash day.

WASH DAY

Every Monday was wash day.
The electric washing machine superceded
the wash boards for scrubbing clothes. Mama
put dirty clothes in the big round enamel
tub on legs. Inside were three
hard rubber paddles attached to a center
cylinder. As they swished back and
forth in the water, they
cleaned the clothes. Attached
above the tub
were two more rubber cylinders
which, when rolling together were designed
to squeeze the water out of
the clothes, as Mama pushed the clothes
between them.
After the clothes were washed or boiled
in the kettle room they got three
rinsings in the galvanized tin
tubs and hung to dry
on the clothes lines behind the wash house.
A washing for a family of eight,
took almost all day,
even though Mama usually
hired someone who lived on our
farm to help.

MAX'S ROOM

After all that building,
Max still didn't have a room of his own.
He was getting
a little uncomfortable
with the sleeping arrangements.
As the only boy
of six children, he had
to share a room with
one and sometimes two sisters.
He grumbled that Sylvia had her own room,
an eight by eight former pantry
off the back porch.
In desperation, Max offered
her twenty-five cents for the room.
That was too much
money for Sylvia to resist.
So she sold her space to Max;
and he finally had a room of his own!

THE MIDDLE ROOM

The "middle room" was so called because
it was the bedroom
between Mama and Daddy's bedroom
at the front of the house,
and the kitchen
at the back of the house.
There, four of us girls slept in two
double beds.
From the ceiling hung a single cord
with a light bulb at the end,
and a short chain
for switching the bulb on and off.
It was the only light source
in the room;
so the one who turned off the light was left
in the dark to get in bed.
Sue got the idea
of tying a string from the chain
to the bedpost
so the light could be turned off
by yanking on the string
from the safety of the bed.
Since the middle room
had no built in closets,
Daddy made a "wardrobe"
without front doors;
and Mama
made a pretty curtain to go across

the front to cover the
clothes.

MAMA'S SEWING

Mama did a lot of sewing for
the family. At one time the sewing
machine was in the middle room
where I slept at that time.
Sometimes as I drifted into sleep,
I could hear the steady droning
of the machine as she pushed the treadle
up and down with her right foot.
Often she sewed deep into
the night to provide clothes for us.
Some of the fabric
she used came from the patterned
chicken feed sacks.
When Daddy came home with
a pickup load of 40 pound bags
of chicken feed, each
of us girls chose the material we wanted.
Mama fashioned delightful versions
of skirts, shorts or dresses for us.
We were quite proud
of our feed sack creations!

MAMA'S GARDENS

In spring Mama's backyard garden came to life.
Beautiful climbing rosebushes
were waves of
color at the entrance.
We were thrilled to take bunches
of sweet-smelling flowers to our teachers.
A picket fence
surrounded the masses of beauty.
A huge mock orange bush grew in a sunny
corner behind splashes of four-O-clocks.
When in bloom, its massive limbs
formed a fountain of white.
Nearby along a stream
of runoff water from the kitchen sink
granddaddy grey beard and
pomgranate bushes grew profusely.
Patches of daffodils, snapdragons, nasturtiums
petunias and marigolds
grew everywhere.
Forsythias, snowball bushes, spirea,
gladiolias and dahlias
grew in other places in the yard.
There was something blooming
all during the spring,
summer and autumn.

SYLVIA AND THE GOSLINGS

Every year Daddy and Mama
had a big vegetable garden in a
small field between our house and the
tenant house. The whole family helped with
chopping and picking the ripe harvest.
The geese helped too.
They picked off the worms and other
insects that ate the leaves
and ruined the plants.
They also had the run of the yard.
One day a goose and her goslings
found a wash tub full of water
in the back yard, so they went for a swim.
Sylvia found them, and decided to join the fun.
Mama discovered her a little while later
shivering in the cold water, playing
with the goslings.
She didn't get punished; but
she got very sick.
Dr. Stanley, our faithful family doctor came.
He said she had pneumonia,
and that she might not live.
He gave her a new medicine called penicillin.
We were all so worried,
we walked around on tiptoes and spoke in whispers
when we were in her room.
In a week or so she was back to
her adventurous self,
except for her blonde curls.

She had lost a lot of her hair because of
the high fever.
The penicillin saved her life!

SYLVIA HAS RHEUMATIC FEVER

Sylvia had another close call
when, at the age of seven,
she contracted rheumatic fever.
One day she began crying with
pain in the joints of her legs.
A fever persisted.
The doctor who was consulted
said she had rheumatic fever and she must
have complete
bed rest for several months.
She could not attend school; but
passed her grade
by studying her lessons in bed.
We all walked slowly around her
and feared we would cause her pain if
we touched the bed.
There seemed to be
a great danger
that she might suffer permanent heart damage.
Shirley was given the
chore of looking after her in the
before and after school hours.
Shirley would carefully dress her,
bring the meals to her,
and attend to many
other needs.
After practically a whole
school year in bed,
Sylvia was able to resume

normal activities,
and never had any heart damage!

Pearl Harbor Bombed

Late one Sunday, on a summer afternoon
when I was seven,
we went to Grandma Lassiter's
house. The grownups talked and we children
played indoors and outdoors:
up and down the big winding stairs
and out on the wrap-
around porch.
Tired of playing,
I went to the living room
with the grownups. I sat down
at a desk in the corner
and played with
the pencils in a small blue vase.
Someone turned on the radio,
and heard the news
that Pearl Harbor had been bombed.
Many had been killed. I didn't know what
all of that meant, but
I could tell the way the grownups talked
that it was very serious.
As their conversation continued, I could
no longer stay awake; and the droning of
their voices put me to sleep.
As Daddy lifted me from the sofa,
I awakened just enough to experience
a sense of security and love in his

arms that would carry me through the war years ahead.

WHEN I THOUGHT I KILLED GRANDMA

On another Sunday all of us went
over to Grandma Lassiter's house.
When we'd come, one of Daddy's brothers
would say, "Here comes Pharaoh's
Army." Everyone would laugh including Mama;
but I could tell she was hurt.
When we got there,
the grownups would gather in the
living room
and discuss the war,
crops, the weather, or politics.
Daddy had three brothers: Bert
Jesse and Russell. They
loved to argue about
politics.
The hotter the argument, the louder
the voices.
It was about that time
when Mama or Aunt Iva
would ask
Grandma a question about some
canning or a kitchen
concoction, to take themselves out of
the fray.
Grandma's house was like a
big playhouse for all of
us grandchildren.
On this particular night, we were playing
"hide and seek".

In trying to find the best place
to hide, I opened Grandma's bedroom door.
To my horror there was Grandma
undressed
to the bare essentials.
She looked at me in despair;
but said nothing, just stood there.
I shut the door and ran
as fast as I could to another
part of the house.
The next day while I was still troubled
about my misadventure,
Daddy and Mama told us that Grandma
had died during the night.
My world caved in. I thought
I had killed Grandma!
Throughout the funeral and the
next several years
I secretly carried that guilt,
Fearing if I told anyone, I would
get the punishment of my life.
Even when I overheard the
whispered words,"heart attack,"
I knew in the secret of
my guilt ridden heart
who had caused it.

SYLVIA, SUE, AND LINDA CRASH THE FUNERAL

On the day that Grandma Lassiter was buried,
Sylvia, Sue, and Linda were considered
too young to attend
the funeral.
They were left at Grandma's house
in the care of a family friend.
Grandma was being buried in
the family cemetery
which was in the middle of a cornfield
not too far from the house.
Sylvia's curiosity got the better
of her; so she took Sue and Linda
and slipped off to
the cornfield.
Some distance from the burial place,
well hidden
by the tall corn stalks,
they crouched low and watched
everything going on
at the gravesite.
As soon as the service was over,
they rushed back to
the house before Mama and Daddy
got there!

THE WAR DRAGS ON

Every day
when Daddy came from
the fields
he turned on the radio at 6:45
and listened to H.V. Kaltenborn,
a news commentator.
I wondered who the "red army"
was, but didn't
ask, for fear they were
heading our way.
Mama was careful when she
used sugar.
"It's rationed", she'd say.
I didn't exactly know
what she
meant; but I knew
it meant less desserts.
When margarine
came from the store
it was white,
until Mama mixed with it
a little package filled with some
gold stuff.
"Why do you do that?" I asked.
"Because of the war," she said.
I didn't understand
what that
had to do with the war.
It still tasted like margarine

to me.
I don' t remember much more
about the war
except the grownups
talked about it a lot.
They seemed very worried.
After listening to the news and
eating supper, Daddy would take a
short rest. Therefore, most of the time
it was dark before he fed and watered
the stock. I loved to watch him light
the kerosene lantern and swing it
back and forth
as he walked to the barn.
One night he came back to the house
with his face covered
in blood. In the dark, he had
fallen onto a pile of tobacco
sticks and cut several
gashes in his face. Mama hurridly
drove him to the hospital when she saw how
badly he was cut. He received several stitches
across his face. We were so happy his eyes
had escaped the splinters.
Even before Daddy was completely healed
from his accident,
he was back to work as usual.
There was plenty of work to be done, even
through winter.
After chores Daddy was always reading something.
He devoured newspapers, political

magazines, and the "Progressive Farmer," which was his favorite farm magazine.

HOG KILLING TIME

The washhouse and kettle room
were command center
on hog killing days.
A very cold winter day was chosen
to kill hogs,
so the meat would not spoil.
Several people helped
Daddy and Mama on the first day.
I was glad to be at school on those days!
After Daddy shot the hogs,
they put them
in a vat of scalding water,
so all the hair on the hogs' skin
could be scraped off.
Next, they were hung by the hind legs
on a scaffold
to let all the blood drain out.
Then Daddy and his helpers
butchered the hogs,
cutting them apart into hams,
shoulders, slabs of bacon,
and other cuts of pork.
With the fat right beneath the skin,
they made cracklings.
To make cracklings, Daddy built a fire
under the big black pot
in the kettle room,
and dumped all the chunks of
cut up fat into the kettle.

When the fire began to heat the fat,
Daddy would stir
the pieces of fat with a big wooden paddle
the size of a boat oar.
The fat would sizzle and shrivel
like dead leaves in winter.
Finally when the crinkled fat was
swimming in hot grease,
Daddy would remove them and squeeze the rest
of the hot grease out through a large
piece of gauze.
All the fat was poured into special metal
tubs. When the fat was congealed
it was called cracklings, and was used in cooking.
A big hog killing
lasted for several days.
Daddy "cured" the meat by "salting it down"
in a big wooden box in the
smokehouse. Later it was taken out
and hung on poles in the smokehouse along with
long strings of sausage, ground pork which
was highly seasoned
and encased in strips of well-cleaned
small intestines from one of the
hogs.
Mama cooked a dish at hog killing time
called "liver hash."
I could never be persuaded to eat it.
However, when Mama made
"crackling biscuits", we were all ready to eat!

ALWAYS CHICKENS

Among other things
Daddy called himself a chicken farmer.
He had hundreds and hundreds
of chickens.
Most of the time he raised
Rhode Island Reds.
They laid a lot of eggs.
Daddy saved most of the eggs to take to the
hatchery. He kept them in wire
baskets in the cool, partially underground
pumphouse which doubled as an egg house.
Each week he packed the eggs into
sturdy cardboard boxes.
Most of the time Daddy could
look at an egg and tell whether it was
big and heavy enough to take to the hatchery.
Sometimes, however, he had to weigh
the egg on a small scale.
Those that didn't pass the test were called "culls,"
which we ate, sold, or gave away.
The larger eggs, which were taken to the
hatchery had to be germ free.
To make sure they were, the chickens
were regularly tested.
Men came from the hatchery and gave each one
a blood test.
All of us children had to catch the
chickens for the test. I fervently hated it!
In all the years we tested chickens, they

never found one with any disease.
What a waste of time!

GATHERING EGGS AND OTHER CHALLENGING ACTIVITIES

It wasn't always easy to get the eggs
from the chicken to the egghouse.
Several challenges
regularly presented themselves.
The first thing that really freaked me out
was when the hen used her nest
for a bathroom.
How lazy can you get?
Trying to find a way to pick up
the egg without coming
into contact with the "eliminated substance"
was the first order of business.
An old rag "came in good" for that.
When the hen was in a family mood,
we called her a "setting hen."
She would protect her eggs
with a fierce peck at the intruding hand.
When a hen decided you had designs
on her eggs, she would grab
a piece of skin and twist. With rage and
revenge, I would grab her whole head
in a death grip with one hand,
steal the eggs with the other,
and make a hasty retreat.
My run-ins were usually with hens;
but once I had an unusual resident in a
nest: a rooster had decided to "try"

to lay some eggs. Day after day
that big burly Rhode Island Red sat on
the nest. Finally he gave up;
but not before he had given the whole
family a good laugh.

I TEACH THE ROOSTER A LESSON

Not all roosters were so docile.
Sometimes they were downright
mean. Some days a particularly
aggressive rooster would
do a little dance
around me,
and try to attack me when
I turned my back.
I defended myself with a five
gallon bucket of feed
I carried.
One day a rooster flew toward me
in a frenzy without a
preliminary dance.
I swung my bucket of mash
knocking him out cold.
I thought I had killed him,
and was already contemplating the
consequences of my action.
However, after lying still a minute or two
he began kicking.
Then he stood up and walked away
while warily watching me
as he retreated.
"I hope you learned your lesson,"
I said out loud as I
breathed a deep sigh of relief.

THE EGG FIGHT

With so many hens laying eggs,
Sylvia and Sue
also had to help gather them.
One cold winter day after school, when
four or five inches
of snow still lay on the ground,
they went to gather eggs.
Each one to a different chicken house.
After finishing the tasks,
both headed toward the house.
For fun, Sylvia threw
a snowball and hit Sue on the head.
Sue returned with the most convenient
thing she could lay her hands on: an egg.
The egg hit Sylvia and spattered,
so the fight was on.
It was over before all the eggs
were thrown;
but still they worried about
what Daddy would say.
They just knew they'd get a whipping!
When Daddy came to the house
later, and found out what
had happened,
he laughed so hard that tears ran down
his cheeks.
And Sue and Sylvia never did
get punished.

BAREFOOT MAX

While Sylvia, Sue and I were
gathering eggs and feeding chickens,
Max was helping Daddy feed the livestock:
mules, hogs, goats, and cows.
He also milked the cow in the morning.
On cold, frosty mornings before the
school bus came, when the moisture in the earth
froze to icy crystals,
Max would grab a milk pail from the kitchen and head
for the barn as barefoot
as if it were summertime.
Mama would say, "Put on your shoes, Max."
"Naw," Max would say, "I'm ok."
And he always was.
Max was so adverse to wearing
shoes that on several
days he slipped by Mama's watchful eye
and went to school barefoot.
The teachers were outraged.
They would have sent him home, had it not been
too far to walk.

SUMMER SOLES

All of us girls liked to go barefoot
too. In spring Mother would not
let us go barefoot outdoors until the leaves
on the trees
got as big as her big toe! We would
watch those leaves; and
when she said it was warm enough,
off came the shoes and socks.
The first few days were painful
because we had lots of
small pebbles in our soil; some were
smooth and some were jagged.
All were painful to tender soles.
Pretty soon the soles of our feet
toughened.
There was a sense of freedom that
came with going barefoot;
but it had its drawbacks.
Once or twice I stuck a nail in my foot
and I'd have to soak it in
salt water. Then Mama would
cover it with Raleigh salve
and a bandage.
Another time when I was going to the chicken house
at noon to gather eggs, without shoes
of course, I almost stepped on a snake
curled up at the entrance!

Nothing, it seemed, would stop me from going barefoot in the summer.

THE BILLY GOAT'S REVENGE

As if chickens, hogs, cattle, and mules
were't enough mouths to feed,
Daddy also had goats!
They usually stayed in the fenced
area between our house
and Uncle Jesse and Aunt Lalia's
house. Max particularly loved
goats. He said when he grew
up he was going to
have a goat farm.
We had one aggressive billy goat
with very large horns.
Max got a big kick out of teasing him.
Max would climb the
gate and run toward the goat
with a stick as if he
were going to strike him.
This made Billy angry;
and he would run after Max.
Max would make a dash for the gate,
and climb over just in time.
One morning Billy must have decided to get
revenge for all that
teasing.
We had walked to the pond at the end
of our road where we caught the school bus
each week day.
Just as we put down our
books with our bag lunches on top,

one of us looked back up the hill,
and saw Billy running toward
us at full speed.
There was no gate to climb,
so we all ran up on the pond enbankment,
which wasn't much of a defense.
We watched in horror as Billy
got nearer and nearer.
When he got to our bus stop
where we had the bag lunches
on top of our books,
he suddenly stopped and began to
tear into our lunches.
Billy was so busy eating our six lunches,
he didn't notice
when we grabbed our books and
dashed to the safety of the
arriving bus.

THE POND

The pond where Billy ate our lunches
was actually an important
part of our lives.
In the summer after working
all the day in the fields, we loved
to go swimming there.
At one end of the pond there was
a good place to go fishing.
Max would go often
but we girls went only
occasionally.
It was not one of our favorite
things to do.
Sometimes in rainy or snowy
weather, Mama or Daddy
would drive us to the bus stop
at the pond, so
we could wait for the
bus in the car.
In winter it could be so cold the
pond would feeze over. While waiting
for the bus, Max and I would
skid rocks across the
ice to see how far they would go.

FISHING IN THE LAKE

Sometimes Max would go fishing in the lake
at the other farm, which
was about two miles away. Actually
it was as much a swamp as it was a lake.
Anyway, Max persuaded Shirley,
Sylvia and me to go
with him. It was
at the far side
of the farm. The closer we got to the
lake, the more we girls wanted
to turn back.
Water oozed above my shoes; and branches
hung almost to the ground.
When we stopped to sink our hooks,
a huge snake slithered off
a fallen log into the water.
After fishing awhile we had caught
plenty of mosquito bites,
but no fish. (Max said we talked too much.)
We also saw
another snake, but still Max persisted,
and we were afraid to return home
without him.
Then all of a sudden a big water
snake lowered his head
from a low slung branch
close to where we stood.
One of us said, "Let's get out of here!"
And we all (including Max)

ran as fast as we could.
That was the one and only time we
went fishing in the
swampy lake!

PIG IN THE BLANKET

Daddy raised a lot of pigs on our farm.
Black pigs, rust colored pigs, and white and black pigs.
Sometimes the sow's cycle and
the weather's cycle
didn't "gee haw." One year
at the first of March when that month
was coming in like a lion, a sow
had her pigs in the middle
of a snowstorm.
Daddy was prepared for just such
an occasion. He had built a farrowing
pen to protect the mama sow and
her newborns. The pen was closed in on
two sides to shut out the driving
north wind and snow.
There was plenty of hay and straw
for coziness. One little piglet, a runt
couldn't find a place at Mama sow's table.
He was about to feeze to death;
so Daddy brought him to the house.
"Let's put him in the oven," Mama said
And so they wrapped him
in a warm blanket and turned on
the oven to less than 100°.
The piglet thawed out, but couldn't return
to the pen. There was nothing left to do
but feed him with a bottle.
We children scrambled to be the first
nurse. By the time that chore got old,

spring arrived and piggy could
hold his own in the litter.

SNOWBALL

One day Daddy brought home an english bulldog puppy.
He was in a shoebox all balled up
like a snowball; so that became his name.
The first night at our house
he cried all night long,
and kept everybody awake.
The more he grew, the uglier he got.
The uglier he got the more
we loved him. He had big sloppy,
slobbery jaws, and bowed legs. He looked
mean and fierce.
But he was as gentle as a kitten to us.
While being our pet, he also helped
Daddy catch stray hogs. Snowball would
catch them by a front or hind leg
and occasionally by the neck. He would
hold on until Daddy could get there.
Once when Mama was alone
and a man walked up and held out his
hand to shake hands, Snowball
grabbed his hand. The man thought
Snowball had practically bitten off
his hand; but Snowball hadn't even broken
the skin.
When Snowball got old and unable to
walk because of the pain of arthritis, Daddy had to
end his life. Daddy shot Snowball in the
wee hours of the morning, so

none of us would see him shed his tears.
That was a sad day for all of us.

GOING TO CHURCH

"Church going" was a once a month ritual
for our family.
The church shared the preacher
with three other churches.
We attended the Clement Primitive Baptist
Church, a small white clapboard
building with no bathrooms,
(only outside toilets)
no Sunday School, or musical instruments.
During the services the women
sat on one side,
and the men sat on the other side.
We sang from a hymn book with only words,
no notes. I guess everyone knew
the tunes by heart.
The minister preached with such a
"sing-song" rhythm I could
not understand
most of what he said.
The best part of going to church was
the occasional dinner on the grounds.
While church attendance was a monthly activity,
religious instruction was daily.
Both Mama and Daddy
lived by the principles and precepts
of the Bible taught to
them by their parents.

SYLVIA AND THE CHINA CABINET

If I had my choice between winter
and summer, I'd choose summer
even though there is much
more work to do in the summertime.
Of course there is one bright spot in winter;
and that's Christmas. We didn't
get a lot of presents, just one or two
things we'd been asking for all year long.
And we always got fruit and nuts.
Every year Daddy bought a bushel basket filled with
oranges, apples, raisins, nuts, and of course, candy.
Mama would fill some of Daddy's old socks
with these goodies for us on Christmas morning.
Mama whipped ivory soap flakes in water
and made "snow" for the Christmas tree.
The lights on the tree were glass candles
filled with a colored liquid
that bubbled when they got warm.
When one by one we found out about the secret
of Santa Claus,
we'd look everywhere for our Christmas
presents. Mama did
a pretty good job of hiding them
most of the time.
However, one year right before Christmas
Sylvia just knew there was
something on top of the china cabinet
in the dining room. So she
opened the glass doors

and started climbing.
Before she could reach her hand
over the top, the whole
china cabinet fell
on top of her.
The upper edge of the cabinet was
caught by the dining table.
By the time the dishes
quit falling out,
Sylvia had vanished.
Between worrying about Sylvia
and agonizing about her heirloom dishes,
Mama was fit to be tied. Of course Mama
was most worried about Sylvia being hurt.
Everyone began looking for her.
While we were searching, several huge airplanes
flew low over the house.
Since an airplane was a rare sight,
We all ran out of the house
to get a glimpse; just in time
to see Sylvia crawling out from under the
front porch to see the planes, too.
And she didn't have a scratch on her!

THE SECRET IS OUT

After Max, Shirley, Sylvia, and I learned
"the secret of Santa Claus."
Shirley said, "Don't tell Sue and Linda,
they're too young to know.
But somehow the secret
leaked out.
One of us snitched
the secret to Sue!
For Sue, such earth shaking news was too
juicy
to keep to herself.
One day soon after, Sue whispered in Linda's ear:
"I've got something to tell you."
After she led Linda to a secluded
place, she said, "Linda, I've got something
terrible to tell you. There's no
Santa Claus!"
Linda burst into tears.
Her world was crushed;
until she learned
she would still get presents
under the tree
on Christmas morning.

LINDA LEARNS TO SHOOT

Linda got the short end of the stick
another time. Max loved
to hunt. He also loved to tease
his younger sisters.
When he got old enough to
hunt with the shotgun, he realized
that when it ejected the
shell, it knocked him back a few steps,
unless he properly steadied himself.
With that knowledge planted
firmly in his mind, he
decided to pull one over on his
youngest sister, Linda.
Now at that time
Linda was about eight years old and small
for her age. Max presented Linda with
the "privilege" of shooting the
big gun into the woods;
and she was thrilled!
Max loaded the gun, placed it on Linda's
shoulder, and gave instructions
to pull on the trigger
as hard as she could.
When the gunshell exploded
out of the barrel
of the shotgun, it knocked Linda
about five feet southward,
flat on her back.
Fortunately for Max, it caused

no visible injuries to Linda; however
some visible ones may have
appeared later on Max's rump.

LINDA LEARNS HOW NOT TO GET CHICKENPOX

When the local epidemic of chickenpox
hit our family, each of us was kept home for
a few days while the
disease ran it course in our body.
Mama would let us lounge
around the house while she served
us milkshakes to help us feel better.
All of that special treatment,
plus getting to stay
out of school for a few days looked
mighty appealing to Linda.
Since Mama warned each of us to stay away from
the one with chickenpox, Linda
decided she wanted chickenpox; and the
best way to get it was to snuggle
right up to the sick
sibling. So after
everyone had gone to bed,
Linda crept into Sylvia's
bed and curled herself around her
chickenpoxed body.
Well, after all that effort,
Linda never did
get the chickenpox!

THE BABY PIGS

One early spring day Mama and Daddy
had to go to the grocery store;
and left us kids at home.
Before they left, Daddy warned us not
to go near the Mama sow who had just had
new baby pigs. "She's very protective of her
babies and might try to hurt you."
"Baby pigs!" The temptation
was too much for Sylvia, Sue, and Linda.
The moment Mama and Daddy left,
they went immediately to see the
pigs. They climbed
over the fence to get a closer look.
Mama Sow decided they had
come too close, and she charged the intruders.
In Linda's haste to get back over
the fence, she caught her bare foot
in the barbed wire that ran across
the top of the fence. One of the barbs
sliced a gash in the bottom of
her foot. Linda limped to the house, crying
all the way. Shirley took care of it as
best she could. She washed the wound and wrapped
it with clean cloths which Mama kept for just
such occasions. When Mama got home she poured turpentine
over the gash, and swabed it with her old reliable
antibiotic cream, Raleigh Salve.

Then she bandaged it tightly.
Soon Linda's foot was as good as new.

"KILLING" RUTH

Shirley tells this story of the time
she thought she had killed me-Ruth.
We were playing and I put my fingers
in the back of the door where
it closes against the door jamb. Whether
intentionally or unintentionally,
Shirley doesn't remember; but
she closed the door on my fingers.
I cried so hard I lost my breath and became
unconscious. I crumpled to the floor
like a rag doll. Shirley was terrified.
She thought she had killed me.
Daddy was at home and came running into the
kitchen where it happened.
As he picked me up, I began to
regain cosciousness.
Shirley was so relieved!

RIDING INSIDE THE TRACTOR TIRE

Sometimes on Sunday afternoons Uncle Bert
and Aunt Lucy, who lived in the town
of Four Oaks,
would come out to visit us.
Their youngest child, Edward Bert
would come to play with us
children. On this
particular Sunday afternoon, Max and
Edward Bert were scrounging around the barn
and came across an old tractor tire
about three feet in diameter. We all took turns
curling up in the center of the tire
and letting someone roll us
around the yard.
What fun it was to roll around and around until
you got so dizzy you'd yell,
"Let me out."
When Edward Bert took his turn
to ride inside the tire,
he let one foot hang out. As he flew
around, Sue got too close,
and "wham!" Edward Bert hit her in the side
of her head, knocking her down.
Her cries were so loud, all the grownups
came running out to see
what had happened.
Sue was not seriously hurt, but
that ended the game.

Much to our chagrin, Uncle Bert
and Aunt Lucy promptly left.

THE OUTDOOR TOILET AND THE SEARS AND ROBUCK CATALOG

Out behind the smokehouse
and down a little
path sat our outdoor toilet.
For me it also served
as a good hideaway.
In a big family one had to have a place
to get away from everybody.
The outdoor toilet provided that
place for me. Often I took a book
I was reading and stayed for awhile.
The toilet was the best excuse for taking a long break.
Besides, there was the Sears and Roebuck catalog;
and it provided two services:
something to read and something to wipe with!
This was a special outdoor toilet,
it was a two-seater;
although I never saw two people using
it at the same time.
The worst thing about the toilet
was that it was outside,
and not much fun to go to in the middle
of the night.
But Mama took care of those emergencies with
a little covered pot!

LINDA STEALS THE SHOW

Sometimes in the evenings we girls
would "put on a show." We liked to dress up
in Mama's old dresses
and shoes. We would sing a solo, recite a poem,
or model clothes.
Shirley usually played background
music on the piano.
Daddy and Mama were our audience.
At one summer evening's "performance,"
it was getting late; and Linda
was told that this was her last time
to perform.
She had wanted to sing "Jerusalem;"
and she also wanted to model
a bathing suit.
She decided to do both at the
same time. So she put on her bathing suit
and sang the song.
The "audience" could hardly
hold back the laughter as their youngest
child belted out the majestic hymn
about the Holy City while modeling a bathing
suit in high heels!

THE INTERVIEW

Mama and Daddy loved to read.
They valued education and always
encouraged us to do our homework and be
good students.
Mama read homemaking magazines and
Daddy read the farm magazines,
especially the "Progressive Farmer."
They both read the
"News and Observer," a daily
newspaper published in Raleigh.
Daddy kept up with the national and world
news by reading "US News and World Report."
All that reading
must have paid off, because
one day a couple of men came
from the local radio station, to interview
Daddy and Mama because of their
successful farming practices.
It was one of the few times we used
the living room.
I could tell Daddy and Mama
felt that this was very important.
They both sat up real straight in their chairs.
The men said that Daddy was a farmer
who didn't put all his eggs in one basket.
For the life of me I couldn't figure
out what that meant.
Anyway, they also published his picture
with an article about him

in the local paper.
We were very proud when friends
and family members
mentioned they had heard the program on the
radio or had seen the picture in the newspaper.

DOODLEBUGS

From the earliest time I can remember,
I saw little funnel
shaped pits in
the sand at the barn or in sandy
areas around the yard.
One day someone told me there
was a doodlebug hiding
at the bottom of the pit in the sand.
This fascinated me and I tried
reaching down and digging him out
but could never get the
doodlebug.
Then I learned to get a small
twig and gently twirl it
around in the pit. The doodlebug,
thinking he'd caught an ant,
would come out of hiding
to get it.
I would then grab him and put him
in the little box I brought with me.
I would sit and stir the sand
in the pits for
hours to see how many doodlebugs
would come out.
While I stirred I chanted,
"Doodlebug, doodlebug,
come and get your
meal."
It was only later I learned

that the doodlebug's real
name is ant lion.

THE LOST CANNISTER SET

Sue tells of the time when she bought
a beautifully decorated red
and white cannister set
for Mama. It was
to be a Christmas present, so she
had to hide it somewhere that
Mama would not go.
She decided to hide it in a large pile
of shelled corn Daddy stored
on the first floor
of the new barn at the bottom of
the hill. He used this corn to feed the
livestock.
When the time came to wrap the
present for Mama,
Sue went to the barn to
retrieve the gift.
Evidently with Daddy getting
buckets of corn from
the pile every day, the "secret
place" had shifted.
Sue clawed into that pile of corn again
and again looking for that cannister set.
She finally found it
just in time for Christmas.

THE JOKE THAT BACKFIRED

Jokes and pokes popped out
like chickenpox on Sylvia. She
loved to have fun any way
she could.
She would walk past one of us
and very innocently poke us on the
shoulder.
Then before you could say
a word, she'd say,
"What'd you hit me for?"
Well, one time the joke backfired!
One day Sylvia dashed into the
kitchen with a
picture she had found in the
"National Geographic Magazine." It
was a full page picture of a
gorilla.
She thrust the picture in front of
Max's face saying, "Look, I
found this picture of you
in a magazine."
Max, without hesitating a second, said,
"No, can't you see? This is a
picture of you!" With that
he stuck it in front of her face.
Sylvia turned and ran
from the room, tasting a bit
of her own medicine.

THE BIGGEST SNOW EVER

Late on a February afternoon the world
turned steel grey. Great white flakes began
to fall from the sky. It snowed all
through the evening, night, and into the next
afternoon. The barn across the road looked
like a giant white cave with two
enormous dark eyes where the
doorless entrances to the stables were.
We felt like characters from Whittier's "Snowbound."
When it finally stopped, we knew there was
enough of the magic white crystals
to keep us out of school for awhile. We
were giddy with joy, except of course, Mama
and Daddy. They were imprisoned in
a house with six overactive schoolchildren!
Daddy shoveled paths to the barn and chicken houses.
We walked through these paths to haul
feed and water to the animals.
Mama hung up snow-wet clothes on chairs
in front of the heater to dry.
She made big batches of snow cream. Eating Mama's
snow cream was about as good as getting
out of school. We would bring her panfuls of
fluffy clean snow. She mixed in creamy milk, sugar
and vanilla flavoring. She scooped it into dessert
dishes for each of us. We ate it while
playing monopoly, Chinese checkers, or rook.
About the third day we were getting "antsy."
We began picking fights with each other, and

thinking rather favorably about school.
That's when Daddy hit upon his idea!
He announced suddenly (out of desperation,
I'm sure) that we were going for a "snow ride."
By the time we bundled into
our warmest (now dry) clothes, Daddy
was waiting outside with a trailer hitched
to the big, red Farmall H tractor.
We piled onto the trailer and
Daddy slowly pulled us all around the yard
and up the road to the neighbors' houses.
Well, it wasn't exactly a sleigh ride;
but it was surely the next best thing.

SETTING OUT TOBACCO PLANTS

In the spring things began to get very busy
around the farm.
One of the first things Daddy did
to prepare for the season
ahead was to plant the tobacco beds. It was
usually in a bottom land where the
soil was fertile and stayed moist most of the time.
After sowing the seeds he covered the bed with
a sheet of thin white gauze to protect
the sprouting plants from late
frosts. When tobacco seedlings were large enough,
we pulled them up and took them to the fields.
We tranplanted the seedlings into long rows.
With ten or more acres, it was a big job.
Daddy gathered the plants and barrels of
water on a trailor pulled by the
tractor. We all hopped on the trailor for a
short ride to the fields.
Once there, we gathered the plants and followed
Daddy down a row. To insert each plant
into the soil, Daddy used a tobacco planter.
This was a metal funnel about waist high.
It had two sections: a larger section to hold
water and a smaller one to "shoot" the tobacco plant
to just the right place in the soil.
The two sections came to a peak at the bottom,
and opened up like a metal mouth to let out a little
water with the plant. One of us followed along beside
Daddy to "shoot" each plant to the soil.

Another sibling followed behind to fill up the
hole made by the tobacco planter. A third helper
kept the planter full of water
from the barrels on the trailor.
Miraculously most of the plants took root and thrived.

THE COUNTRY STORE

Daddy's cousin, Robert Adams
owned a country store about two miles
from our house. It was perched in a "Y"
where two roads diverged and continued downhill.
I often wondered what kept the store from
tumbling downhill onto the roads. It
never did, of course.
The dirt floors were covered with sawdust
and emanated a special kind of smell
that mingled the scents of of molassas, chewing
tobacco, cigarette smoke and candy.
On days when we had worked hard in the fields,
Daddy would allow us to go with him to the store.
We would all pile into the big old buick roadster
and "take off."
Cousin Robert sold molasses from a big wooden barrel.
Molasses was so yummy on Mama's homemade
biscuits, I'm sure that was why I began
to look like a butterball
by the time I was in the fifth grade.
It was at this store we met the
bookmobile in the summertime. We all
loved to read, and we'd get a big stack to last
until the next time the bookmobile stopped.
Not only did we judge a book by its cover,
but also by its smell. A book had to pass my
"smell test" before I would choose it.
Sue says she can still remember
the smell of some of those good books.

While at the store we would get
cold carbonated drinks:
refreshing grape, orange or
coca cola so strong it made our eyes
and noses burn.

FAMILY TRIP TO THE BEACH

With the multitude of summer work
on the farm, there was
no such thing as a "vacation." *So*
imagine how thrilled we were when Mama
and Daddy decided to take us to the
beach for the day.
It took a lot of preparation.
First, what about bathing suits for
five girls?
Mama had figured out that one.
She simply made them out of pretty, bright
material. They were gathered at the shoulder,
at the waist, and at the top of
each leg with elastic. They looked
like a kind of romper suit!
Sue was afraid that when she got in the
water, all the elastic would come
loose. Luckily, that did not happen.
On the day of the much anticipated trip, we all
rose early. Mama packed a big basket
of fried chicken, biscuits, cake
and condiments; and we
took off.
Before we got to the beach, we stopped
at a country church. It was deserted, because it
was not Sunday. We spread our lunch
and ate on the outdoor homecoming picnic
benches.
We did get to the beach; and for the

first time, saw the shore of the Atlantic Ocean.
We came home to nurse our sunburns
and enjoy the sweet memories of a good time
on our first vacation.

Max and his best friend, Hampton
Langdon

Ruth with cousin Peggy Creech

Ruth as an 8th grader.

Mama in the yard with Ruth, Sue,
Shirley, and Linda.

THE DROUGHT

Almost every summer, at one time
or another, we worried about not having
enough rain.
One summer when it was drier than usual,
Daddy said,"If it doesn't rain soon
the late garden won't come up;
the corn and cotton won't 'make';
the tobacco will dry up in
the fields, and there
will not be enough
money to buy feed for the chickens,
and the hogs, or fertilizer
for next year's crop."
We could tell Daddy was very
worried. That made us children worry too.
We all prayed for rain, and searched
the sky every day for the tiniest cloud.
When finally it did rain, we children would
run out into the downpour and splash
in puddles until Mama
called us in for fear we'd catch
colds. Another one of my favorite things
to do when it rained and we couldn't
work in the fields,
was to run into the bedroom where
I slept; lie across the bed and read,
or just listen to the soothing
sound of rain on the tin roof.
Every year during a time of drought,

it seemed to rain
just before it was too late!

THE DUST STORM

Even though the rains did not come,
There was still a lot
of work to do in the fields.
Grass must be chopped
out of the rows of cotton plants,
tobacco plants, and
sometimes out of the corn.
The hot dry ground burned my bare
feet. Mama made
us wear straw hats
when we left the house. I
hated a straw hat and would pull
mine off before I got
to the field.
My face turned as red as a beet,
whether I had a hat on
or not.
As we chopped, Max, Shirley, Sylvia
and I talked about what
we would do
when we were all grown up.
One particularly hot, dry day,
Max said suddenly, "Look at the sky!"
The whole sky was an inferno.
It looked as if we were
inside a red globe.
Max said, "I think it's the end of the world!"
I threw down my hoe, and raced
back toward the house.

Max, Shirley, and Sylvia were
right behind me.
Before we could get to the house,
a wall of blowing dust enveloped us.
Our eyes, our clothes,
our mouths were full of it.
As we neared the house, we saw Mama
driving home from a neighbor's
house as fast as she could, and yelling
as she got out of the car,
"Shut the windows,
close the doors!"
Even then the dust covered everything
in the house.
Mama huddled with all of us
in the kitchen in front
of the refrigerator. The wind grew stronger and
the house began to "rattle."
Suddenly she said, "Move, the refrigerator
might fall on us."
The wind was howling so fiercely,
we could hardly hear each other
yell.
"What is it, Mama?" we asked.
Mama didn't answer, she was worried about
Daddy getting home safely
from a far field with a mule and plow.
Just then through a window, we
saw Daddy coming. The mules
were pulling the plow
so fast Daddy could hardly

keep up.
Molly and Maud galloped straight
to the barn.
Finally, the wind died down,
and Daddy was safe inside the house.
But everything was covered
with dust.
Even the dishes inside the cabinets
were dusty, and had
to be washed.
The corn stalks
were lying flat in the fields.
The next day we all went to
the fields to set up stalks of corn
and push dirt around the roots.
The tobacco was blown over too,
and had to be set upright.
It took many days to repair the damage
of a half hour of wind.

THE TORNADO

As damaging as a dust storm is,
a tornado is even more
destructive.
Once a small tornado
touched down on our farm.
It blew off the roof
of our chicken house and lifted
the chickens right out of the
nests.
Its swirling winds deposited
those chickens down at
the pond one half mile away.
Some landed in the water,
and others around the
edge of the pond.
The bewildered chickens in the pond
managed to climb ashore.
They were all caught
and brought back
safely.
The tornado also demolished Uncle Russell's
tenant house,
blowing the roof and its contents
into our field a mile away.
Miraculously no one was hurt.
Daddy said we had a lot
to be thankful for!

SUCKERING TOBACCO

Of all the chores on the farm
I hated suckering tobacco
the most.
It was the stickiest, gooiest job
I ever had the privilege
to hate.
The suckers grew out of the
stalks of tobacco where
the leaf and the
stalk were joined together.
They must be pulled out because
they would keep the leaves
from getting large
and lusciously gold when
cured.
To make the job even
worse
we had to kill the big, green, horned
tobacco worms when we
found them.
Sometimes Sue just put them
in a jar with a lid
and let Daddy kill them later.
For me it was easier
just to "squash" them right
there.
At the end of the day
we were covered with a black,
sticky substance

that was murder to get off.
Then Mama would give us tomato peelings
to help remove the gook.
And they worked!

TOBACCO BARNING TIME

Plant by plant
row by row
the tobacco finally became
ready to harvest.
Harvesting tobacco, getting it from
the field to the barn and
and preparing it to be cured
was called "barning."
It was an intensive
six-week chore.
Everyone got tired and grumpy.
On some days our morning
began at 4 A.M.
Because the cured tobacco
must be taken out of the barn
before the day's "barning" began,
Mama would call us at
that unmerciful hour when it was
still dark and our moods
were darker.
We walked like zombies to the
barn where
Daddy already had the tractor and trailer
waiting.
Stick by stick
we filled the bed of the trailer
with cured tobacco.
We took the sticks of tobacco
to the packhouse

where we unloaded them.
When we finished, we had worked up
a real appetite!
Mama had a breakfast of
scrambled eggs, sausage
and freshly
baked biscuits with butter and jelly.
It was almost worth all
that work.
After breakfast, we headed back
to the barn shelter
for the regular day of
barning tobacco.
All day Max, Daddy and a couple
of other men
had the backbreaking job
of pulling the tobacco leaves off
the stalk. This was
called "cropping" the tobacco.
The croppers placed the
bundles of green
tobacco into a tobacco sled.
The sled was pulled by one of our mules,
usually Molly.
Sylvia "drove" the sled back and forth from
the barn to the field.
One day, Sylvia left the barn
with the empty sled.
In a few minutes we heard her yelling,
"Whoa, Molly, whoa," at the top of her voice.
We looked up and there was Sylvia standing

on the back of the sled, pulling the reins as hard
as she could;
and Molly pulling the sled,
and galloping as fast as she could.
They were heading
straight for the barn shelter.
When Molly reached the shade of the
shelter,
she suddenly stopped.
We figured she had been spooked by something,
or just reckoned she could
stand the sun no longer, and decided
to hurry back to the shelter.
Other than a little shocked and weak,
Sylvia was as good as new.
She promptly coaxed Molly back to the field.
The next time, she brought a full sled
of tobacco leaves.
The leaves were carefully laid
on a bench where we picked up two or three
at the time and handed them
to a "stringer" who looped the bundle
with twine, and tied it
to a tobacco stick about four feet long.
The sticks of green
tobacco were then hung upon racks
adjoining the tobacco barn.
At lunch we took a two hour break.
Mama always had
a big meal waiting for us.
She usually had fried chicken, pork chops

or beef stew; which
she served with several vegetables:
field peas, corn, beets, cabbage,
butterbeans, or string
beans, along with a big pan
of cornbread and a bowl
of diced tomatoes
spiced with vinegar and sugar.
Daddy always said those tomatoes
gave the peas a "college education."
Mama never failed to have a
delicious dessert; banana pudding,
sheet cake, or rice pudding.
After lunch we took
a much needed nap. Daddy
always called us at 2 o'clock sharp
to get back to work.
Sometimes we finished after dark.
Four a.m. seemed a long time ago. We would
be almost too tired and sleepy to eat.
But Mama always made us wash
our faces, hands and especially our
dusty feet in basins of warm sudsy water
before we came into the house.
At that time of day between sunset
and dark, the whipperwills would be calling.
Mama would say, "Listen to the whipperwills.
They are singing, 'Wash your feet, wash
your feet.'"

THE BEATING

During the long days of barning tobacco
fatigue built up, day upon day. Some days we
barned tobacco at our house. On other days
we went to a neighbor's house
and helped them, so when it was our day
again, they would help us. There might
be fifteen or twenty people getting
sticky and gummy together as we handled the
leaves of green tobacco.
Fatigue would sometimes breed disagreements
and short tempers.
There was a young lady from a neighboring farm
who helped us. She usually brought her five year
old boy with her. He was tiny for his age, pale
and undernourished-looking. His mother told
him to stay around the barn, and not go
out of sight. One day he evidently
wandered too far. His mother stopped working,
went after him and dragged him back
to the barn shelter. As she got in view
of the others, she picked up a piece of sturdy
tobacco stick and began beating and berating
him. Instead of yelling at the top of his
voice, he emitted the most pitiful
whimpering sound I had ever heard. It sounded
like an animal caught in a trap.
This gross abuse burned an indelible imprint

upon my mind. One which time would not alter or fade.

CURING TOBACCO

After the green tobacco was hung
in the barn,
the process of curing began.
Daddy would build a roaring fire at
the mouth of the furnace
which ran like a big
cement monster
across the center floor of the barn.
As the fire and smoke thundered through
the furnace, the heat
permeated the racks and racks
of green leaves. It reached to the
rafters some twenty feet high.
The rich, pungent, humid
scent of curing
tobacco filled the summer air
of our farm.
To keep the intense heat flowing
through the tobacco,
Daddy would often spend
the night at the barn. The hoped-for result
was dry, leathery,
golden-yellow tobacco leaves
that would demand
a high price at the market in Smithfield.

GRADING TOBACCO AND LISTENING TO THE WORLD SERIES

The last step before selling the tobacco
at the warehouse in Smithfield
was grading it.
Daddy constructed a long bench
which was divided into sections with
tobacco sticks stuck into holes.
He and Mama put the best golden leaves in the first
section. The medium grade went into the next section,
and the darker leaves were put into a third
section. The brown, broken pieces were trash
and were thrown away.
When all the tobacco in one load
was graded, it was tied into bundles
of eight to ten leaves with one soft golden leaf
wrapped around the top to hold the leaves
together. It was then ready for the market.
While Mama and Daddy were
confined to the packhouse grading tobacco,
they listened to the baseball World Series.
(I always had a feeling Daddy timed it just right
to be grading tobacco during the World
Series, because he was a
big baseball fan.)
He often took us to see the Smithfield team play
in the Tobacco League.
It was a special family evening together,
and sometimes Mama would accompany us.

I got crushes on the baseball players;
and daydreamed about meeting them and
sweeping them off their feet with the
first look at me.
Of course that never happened!

... AND BASKETBALL

Another sport that was dear
to my family's heart was basketball.
The first basketball goal was
nailed to a big oak
tree in the side yard. Roots
kept deflecting the
basketball, so it was moved
to the front of the garage above the
wide open entrance.
But there the dirt proved to be
too sandy, so finally Daddy
and Max moved it to the new barn which had
been built in a large scooped-out area
we called the "clay pit."
There Max, Sylvia, Sue and I practiced whenever
we could.
All four of us got on the Four Oaks High School
girl's or boy's basketball teams during our
high school years.
Max, Sue and I played OK, I guess. Let's
just say we didn't break any
records.
But Sylvia, on the other hand was
an outstanding player.
She was tall, fast and had a mean
left hook!
For many years she held
the record for

the most points in one game
for our county.

PICKING COTTON

The next big job after harvesting the tobacco
was picking cotton. Again, except
for Mama, it was a whole-family affair.
Each year Daddy planted several large
fields of cotton. It was ready
to be picked when the boll holding the
cotton inside burst open and dried
to reveal four needle-sharp
points. Nestled in the bosom of
the boll, was a fluffy white ball of cotton.
A field of ready-to-pick cotton looked
like a field of clean white snow.
Well, it may have looked like snow; but
it definitely didn't feel like snow.
Picking the cotton
out of the bolls was a "needling" job
for my tender fingers. My fingers
got so raw I would put on gloves; however
that slowed down the amount I could pick.
I wanted to pick 100 pounds a day because
Daddy gave each of us $1.00 if we picked
that amount in one day.
To hold the cotton we picked, we dragged
a burlap sack held by a strap which
stretched across one shoulder.
At the the end of a round of two rows,
we would empty our sack onto our
own burlap sheet. At the end of the day
Daddy weighed each sheet of cotton. Once

when I was a couple of pounds shy of
100 pounds, I began to cry, because I knew
I would not get a dollar. But Daddy gave
me a dollar anyway. Daddy was really
a softie at heart.
It seemed we were always picking
cotton during our Thanksgiving holiday.
Once when we were grumbling about
ruining our Thanksgiving vacation,
Daddy said smugly, "We're going to 'knock off'
in a little while and go to the house, so
just be patient." (knock off was Daddy's
term for quitting for the day.)
When we went to the house, we found
Mama fixing a big Thanksgiving dinner
with all the trimmings!

Sylvia in her basketball uniform.

Sylvia, Sue and Linda on the staircase

All five sisters in the yard.

OUR TEENAGE YEARS

As each of us entered the teenage years
we developed special interests
and talents.
When Max began to like science
and related subjects,
he changed from wanting to be
a goat farmer
to wanting to be a doctor.
Shirley revealed a talent
for organizational,
diplomatic, and mathmatical skills.
She wanted to do something
in the business or teaching area.
I was a more introverted
person and leaned
toward interests such as reading,
writing, and a hunger for the
knowledge of God.
Sylvia blended together
personality,
athletic, and writing skills.
She was a real people
person, and like Daddy, she never
saw a stranger.
Sue was a mixture of athletic ability,
personality,
and inventiveness. She was always
thinking up new
ways of doing things.

Sue was also an avid reader and read
anywhere
she could find a quiet spot.
She even read under the
the shade trees in the fields
at the end
of the corn or tobacco rows
while waiting to
fill the fertilizer distributor for
Daddy, who was driving
the tractor.
Linda got along well with everyone.
She had a very sweet, positive
personality,
and a servant heart.
Those talents
led her into the field of nursing.

MAX GOES TO COLLEGE

Max was the first one of us to leave home.
He entered
Mars Hill College in the fall of 1947.
After being there for two years
he went to Wake Forest College
and graduated in 1951.
He studied hard in those years;
but there were
lots of fun times too.
One Halloween a group of male
students "borrowed" a
farmer's cow, and managed to get
her up the elevator to the
top floor of the
girl's dorm.
The boys hid somewhere and
watched. The girls screamed as if
they'd never seen a cow before.
After graduating from
Wake Forest College, Max
applied to several medical schools.
Meanwhile he worked on the
farm for the summer, cropping tobacco,
chopping grass, feeding the
animals around the farm,
and waiting for an answer to his
applications.
Finally one hot summer day
when Max was chopping grass,

a letter came from Bowman Gray
School of Medicine in Winston-Salem, N.C.
The letter was brought to Max.
After taking a deep breath,
Max read the letter …
Then he threw his hoe so far into
the air, it took "awhile"
to come down.
It took a while for Max to come
down from his "cloud nine" too.
However, there were harder
days of study ahead.

COLLEGE YEARS CONTINUE

By the time Max graduated from college,
Shirley had already finished
two years at Flora McDonald College;
and headed to East Carolina
College to finish
her business degree in teaching.
At that time I was already
at East Carolina
studying to be either a language arts
teacher,
or a librarian.
So when Shirley joined me at college,
I persuaded her to room with me.
(As if we hadn't already had
enough "togetherness" growing up in
the same family.)
The year I graduated, Shirley had finished
her first year of teaching High School
business in Burlington, North Carolina.
Meanwhile Sylvia had begun her first
year at East Carolina.
Only Sue and Linda were left
on the farm
to help with all the chores …

Max in medical school.

Daddy with daughters Sue, Sylvia, Shirley, and Ruth.

Linda in nurse's uniform.

Ruth in a parade at East Carolina College.

DADDY HAS A HEART ATTACK

In February of that year, 1956,
I was struggling through student
teaching in high school language arts.
One afternoon while I was in the
college library preparing
for the next day's
lessons,
Mama was welcoming Daddy home
from a day of planting
tobacco beds. He was preparing
for the new season
of spring planting. He mentioned
to Mama that he didn't feel
well; one shoulder
and arm were hurting.
He sat down at the table to talk
to Mama while she cooked
supper.
Linda was helping her
while Sue studied her French
lessons.
Suddenly in the middle of a sentence,
Daddy collapsed onto the table
and then fell out of his chair
onto the floor.
While Mama tried to revive him,
she yelled for Linda and Sue
to get Uncle Jesse and
Uncle Grover.

Uncle Jesse and Aunt Lalia
lived just up the dirt road from us.
Linda ran as fast as she could
and rode back with Uncle Jesse
to the house.
Uncle Grover and Aunt Iva,
Daddy's sister, lived about a mile
away. Sue ran there to tell
them. They went first to Daddy's cousins,
Gladys and Irving Langdon,
who had a phone. There they called
Dr. Alderman, Daddy's physican.
Before the doctor came,
Uncle Jesse tried to resuscitate Daddy,
but to no avail.
Dr. Alderman determined that
Daddy had probably died
immediately upon falling to the floor.
The next day we were all in a kind
of twilight zone; we knew with
our minds that Daddy was
gone, but our hearts refused
to accept the fact.
Someone moved most of the
furniture out of the front bedroom,
so Daddy's body could be
placed there after the preparations
for burial had been completed.
On the day of the funeral, as I stood
looking at Daddy in the satin-lined coffin,
surrounded by beautiful flowers

from family and friends, I felt
as if I were in a dream.
Daddy's body was taken to Pisgah Church
for the funeral. As we drove
out of the driveway to attend the funeral,
we all saw a brilliant rainbow
stretched across the cloudless sky
above the packhouse. When we returned to
the house after the funeral, we were
marveling about seeing the rainbow on such a
sunny day. Someone in the family
remembered that the rainbow was mentioned
in the Bible. We got the family Bible
and found the passage in Genesis 9:13–17.
To our amazement the words had
been underlined with a bold
pencil mark.
We questioned each other, and
no one remembered having ever
looked up that passage,
and certainly not underlining it.
We thought surely Daddy must
have marked that scripture
during one of the times he was
reading the Bible.
Then Mama told us that she
had asked God to let
her know in some small way that
Daddy was in heaven;
and now she knew that he

was with the Lord.
The rainbow was her sign!

THE TIME AFTER ...

After Daddy's death Mama continued
to manage the farms with skill
and courage.
Haywood and Vernelle Sanders lived
in the nearest tenant house.
They stayed to farm the land
and help Mama in many ways.
Sue and Linda were still in high school.
Sylvia came home from college at
the end of the semester, and stayed
to help with the farm chores and prepare
for her marriage to Larry Woody, an
Air Force Marine officer from
Texas.
When Sue entered college at East Carolina
to prepare to be a teacher and later a librarian
and Linda entered Bowman Gray School of Nursing
the following year, Mama was left at home
to manage all by herself.
She downsized the stock, and rented
out some of the land, but continued to
handle the day to day business of
farming singlehandedly.
She helped each of us financially so we
could stay in college.
Max graduated from Bowman Gray School
of Medicine and married Laura Pope,
a music teacher.
After serving two years in the army, Max

joined a medical practice in Danville, Virginia.
Sue and I graduated from East Carolina
College and became teachers (and later librarians)
Linda became a registered nurse.
Eventually we all married and reared eighteen
grandchildren. Mama continued to live
on the farm and manage the farms until she
was ninety-seven years old.
At that time she "retired" to an assisted
living facility in Smithfield called
Meadowview which doesn't have a view
of a meadow but has a big front porch with
a view of a busy street where she and
her friends and family can sit and
enjoy the world passing by!

The road that runs through the farm was later paved

In the packhouse tobacco was stored and graded.

Uncle Grover and Aunt Iva's house on a hill beyond pond, fields and cows.

The pond at the end of the road where we met the school bus.

Mother at 100 years old.

We celebrate Mama's 80th birthday.

Appendix

APPENDIX: MAMA'S FAVORITE RECIPES

ICEBOX FRUIT CAKE

1 lb. marshmallows

1 lb. dates

1/2 lb. english walnuts 1/2 lb.

pecans

1 can sweet condensed milk

1 lb. graham crackers

Cut up together: marshmallows, dates and nuts.
Pour into this mixture the sweet condensed milk. Crush the
graham crackers up fine and work into the mixture of fruit,
nuts and milk. Pack down in a deep buttered dish or pan and
let chill overnight. Turn out, wrap in foil and slice as needed.
keep refrigerated.

JAPANESE FRUIT CAKE

1 C. butter

2 C. sugar

3 C. flour

1 fresh coconut, grated

1 C. pecans

4 Tsp. baking powder

JAPANESE FRUIT CAKE (Continued)

1 C. milk

6 eggs

1 box raisins

2 tsp. cinnamon

1 tsp. ground cloves

1 tsp. nutmeg

Cream butter, add sugar and mix thoroughly. Add unbeaten eggs, one at a time. Beat each one in thoroughly before adding the next. Sift dry ingredients together and add them alternately with milk. Finally add coconut, nuts & flour-covered raisins. Pour into 4 greased round cake pans. Bake in 350 degree oven for about 30 minutes. Cool and put together with filling.

FRUIT CAKE FROSTING

2 C. sugar

2 lemons

2 oranges

1 box coconut

4 Tbs. flour

Mix sugar & flour. Cut oranges & lemons into small bits.(not rinds) Cook together until consistency of honey. Add coconut. Cook 2 minutes. Cool and put between cake layers & top.

MAMA'S RICE PUDDING

1 C. leftover cooked rice

1½ C. whole fresh cow's milk

¼ C. fresh cream butter

1 C. raisins

2 C. water

1¼ C. sugar

3 eggs

pinch cinnamon

Combine rice, ½ C. of the milk, sugar, and butter in a saucepan. Bring just to a boil. Beat eggs into remaining milk: Slowly blend into cooked mixture. Bring back to a boil, stirring often. Remove from heat and add the rice and raisins. Makes 8 servings.

BUTTER ROLLS

2 C. self rising flour

1 C. buttermilk

1/2 C mixture of cinnamon & sugar

hand full of lard

3 or 4 Tbs butter

Thoroughly mix flour, lard and buttermilk in a large wooden bowl until it forms a soft ball of dough. Continue to knead the dough for a few seconds. Place ball of dough on surface which has flour sprinkled on it. With a rolling pin, roll the dough into a large circular form 1/4 " thick. Sprinkle the sugar/cinnamon mixture evenly over the surface of the dough. Pinch off small pieces of butter and dot over dough. Carefully roll up the dough and cut into about 1/2 " pieces with a sharp knife. Place into a greased biscuit pan and bake in 400 degree oven about 12–15 minutes, or until lightly brown on top. Bush tops with melted butter. (optional)

The whole family about 1945

978-0-595-47263-5
0-595-47263-X

CPSIA information can be obtained
at www.ICGtesting.com
Printed in the USA
LVHW091051010420
651840LV00024B/825